Mr Pusskins

Bunnykins the Beautiful

For the lovely ladies Liz and Giselle,
without whom this book wouldn't exist!

DESIGN AWARD

With her excellent eye for detail and her amazing computer skills, Giselle Gimblett received the trophy for 'Best Designer on the Planet' at a glittering award ceremony last night.

EDITORIAL AWARD

After years of dedication and wordy brilliance, Liz Johnson has won the top award of 'Best Editor in the World'. Her acceptance speech moved many to tears.

ORCHARD BOOKS

338 Euston Road, London NW1 3BH

Orchard Books Australia

Level 17/207 Kent Street, Sydney, NSW 2000

First published in 2008 by Orchard Books

Text and illustrations © Sam Lloyd 2008

The right of Sam Lloyd to be identified as the author and illustrator
of this work has been asserted by her in accordance with the Copyright,
Designs and Patents Act, 1988.

A CIP catalogue record for this book is available from the British Library.

ISBN 978 1 84616 524 5

1 3 5 7 9 10 8 6 4 2

Printed in China

Orchard Books is a division of Hachette Children's Books, an Hachette Livre UK company.

www.hachettelivre.co.uk

BEST-LOOKING PET

Mr Pusskins

BEST IN SHOW

Sam Lloyd

ORCHARD BOOKS

This is the story of a little girl called Emily,
and her dear cat, Mr Pusskins.

One morning, while flicking through the
paper, Emily spotted something — there was
a pet show in town that very day!

PET SHOW
COMES TO TOWN

Bring along your beloved pet to be judged by our panel of top experts. Please bear in mind that standards will be very high and only the finest of pets may enter. Contestants must be one year and over.

"Oh, Mr Pusskins! You're such a handsome boy, you simply must enter!" gushed Emily.

But Mr Pusskins wasn't so keen . . .

Little Whiskers, Emily's dear kitten,
was too young to enter the competition.
"We can both support Mr Pusskins instead,"
said Emily, excitedly.
Mr Pusskins glared at the other contestants.
Why did they look so snazzy for such
a silly show?

But as soon as Mr Pusskins entered the arena, he knew it was because of . . .

....the
TROPHY!

It was the most fabulous thing Mr Pusskins had ever seen. He simply **had** to have it!

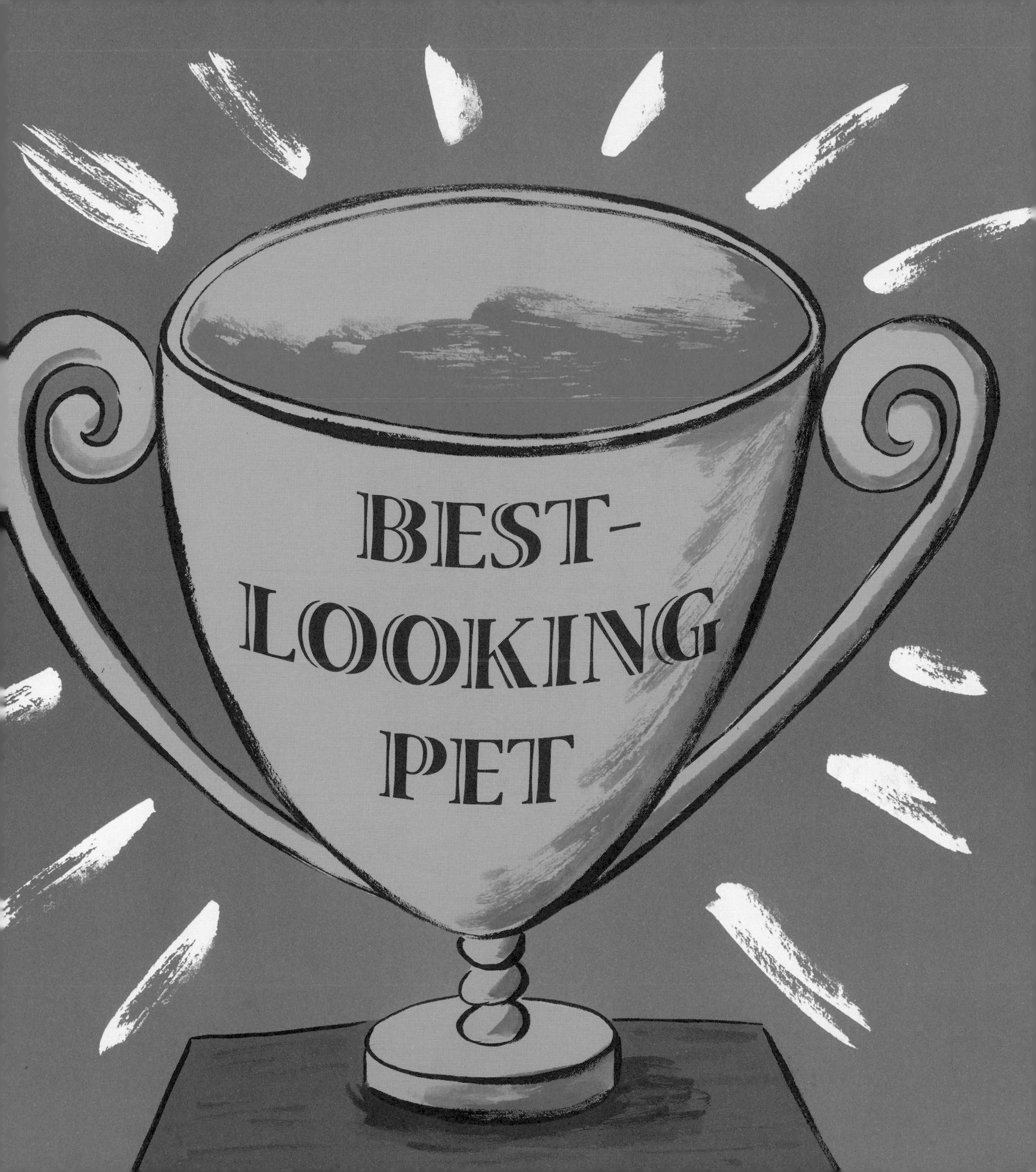
BEST-
LOOKING
PET

He hurried to the
dressing room,
where . . .

he licked . . .

and slicked . . .

and buffed and fluffed . . .

. . . until he was **magnificent!**

When Mr Pusskins joined the other pets they gasped in amazement. Surely he'd win and the trophy would be his!

Just then, they heard an announcement . . .

Mr Pusskins wondered where the
judging would take place – luckily
Madame Fifi seemed keen to
show him where to go.

Mr Pusskins raced off. There was not a
moment to lose. He must win the competition
and get his paws on that trophy! Madame Fifi
trotted away in the other direction.

But hang on, this wasn't where he should be! Drat! That dirty, double-crossing poodle must have tricked him!

Mr Pusskins had to get to the judging – fast!
He needed to take a short cut.

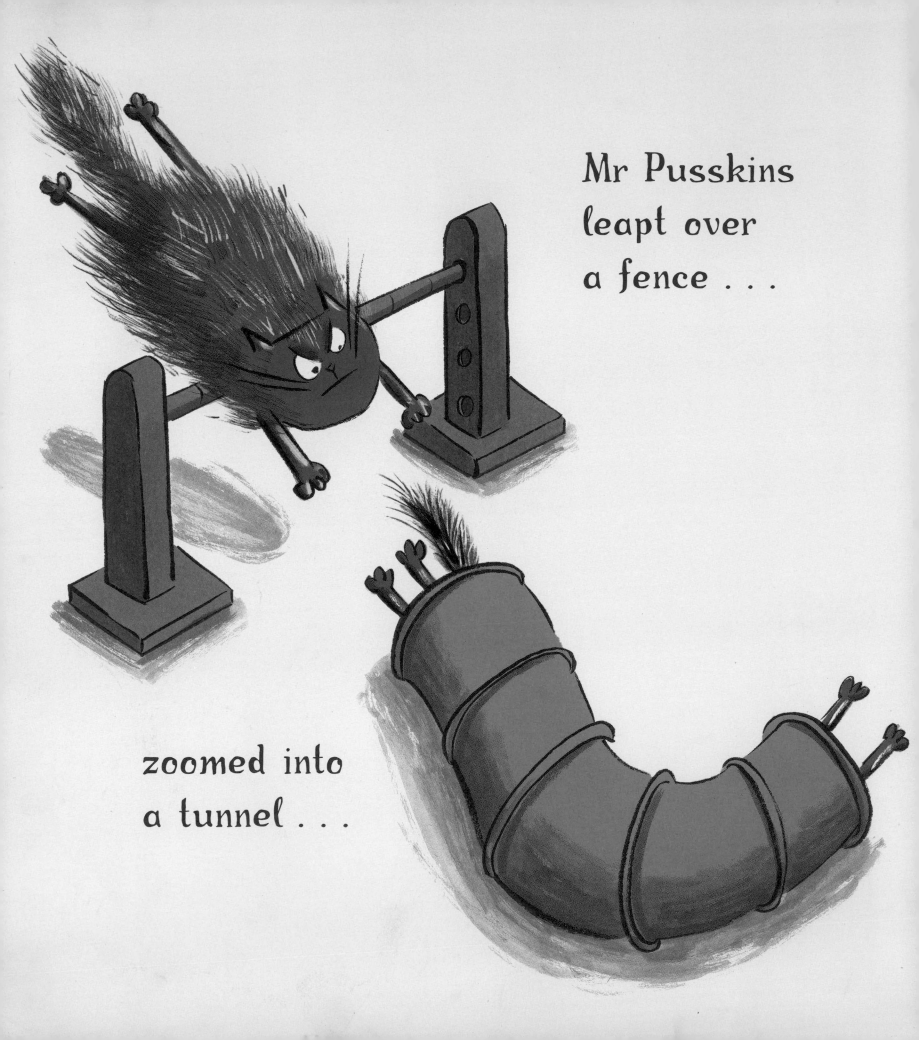

Mr Pusskins leapt over a fence . . .

zoomed into a tunnel . . .

zipped between
some flags . . . .

pounced through
a hoop . . . .

. . . and arrived at the judging, just in time.
He hoped no one would notice his mishap!

Mr Pusskins waited anxiously. He wanted that trophy so much.

Finally, the announcement was made.

"And the winner is ..."

". . . MADAME FIFI FOU-FOU!"
TROUBADOUR THE TRIUMPHANT
BUNNYK THE BEAUTIFUL
BEST-LOOKING PET
MR PUSSKINS
MADAME FIFI FOU-FOU

Mr Pusskins was **mortified**.
He couldn't bear to watch his precious
trophy go to that **cheating** dog.
He had to find Emily and tell her everything.

Emily squeezed Mr Pusskins tight.
"There, there, darling. Never you mind,"
she soothed. "We both know Madame Fifi
didn't deserve to win."
Suddenly, there was another announcement!

"Mr Pusskins
has won the Top Talent Trophy!"

"Mr Pusskins! The way you zipped through
the obstacle course was incredible!"
exclaimed the judge. "Please accept
our most spectacular Top Talent Trophy!"
Mr Pusskins purred with pleasure.

This is the end of the story of a little girl called Emily, and her dear cat, Mr Pusskins. Even though the trophy is in pride of place . . .

Emily doesn't need it to prove how wonderful
Mr Pusskins is . . .

because she's always known!

Troubadour the Triumphant

Monsieur de la Stick

Madame Fifi Fou-Fou